MIC

SQUIDGE
DIBLEY

DESTROYS
THE SCHOOL

LOTHIAN
Children's Books

FOR LOU

A Lothian Children's Book
Published in Australia and New Zealand in 2019
by Hachette Australia
Level 17, 207 Kent Street, Sydney NSW 2000
www.hachettechildrens.com.au

10 9 8 7 6 5 4 3 2 1

 A catalogue record for this book is available from the National Library of Australia

ISBN 978 0 7344 1942 2

Cover design by Amy Daoud
Cover illustration by Mick Elliott
Text design by Amy Daoud
Author photograph courtesy of Melissa Mai
Printed and bound in Australia by McPherson's Printing Group

 **MIX** Paper from responsible sources FSC® C001695

The paper this book is printed on is certified against the Forest Stewardship Council® Standards. McPherson's Printing Group holds FSC® chain of custody certification SA-COC-005379. FSC® promotes environmentally responsible, socially beneficial and economically viable management of the world's forests.

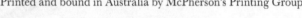

CHAPTER 1

The first time I saw Squidge Dibley, his face was squashed against the classroom window.

It's a third-storey window.

Squidge popped up like a piece of toast from a toaster, as if this was **a totally normal thing** to happen on a random Wednesday morning at Craglands South Primary School.

He blinked at me. I blinked back at him. Suddenly I understood what our class fish, Bubble O'Gill, must feel like when we stare into his fish bowl.

In that moment, I had a preview of the _full-scale weirdness_ that was about to come. I'm talking EPIC, EXPLOSIVE, INEXPLICABLE WEIRDNESS that would change our lives forever.

I didn't know it was Squidge Dibley then. All I knew was that it was impossible for **anyone's** head to be at that window unless they were standing on a ladder, or hanging from a helicopter, or were some sort of half-spider creature.

Squidge pressed his face against the glass and smiled at me, like there was nothing unusual about peering through a third-storey window.

In the split second before everyone spun around to see what the commotion was, Squidge Dibley was gone.

Nobody had seen him except me.

This was just the beginning.

Actually, it was the beginning of the end of all the stuff that happened, so I need to go back to the beginning of the beginning, before the stuff that happened at the end happened.

Here goes.

This is me.

My name is Padman O'Donnell.

People call me **Pad** for short, which is annoying, because there are so many **not awesome** things called pad.

Sometimes people call me **PandaMan** to be funny, but it's not funny at all. It just sounds like a lazy, overweight superhero.

Mum says that Padman is a totally normal name in Sri Lanka and that if you walk down any street there, you'll bump into a Padman soon enough.

Anyway, that's my name and I had to say it because a really good teacher told me that a narrator – that's ME – should tell everyone something about themselves so the person reading – that's YOU – knows who's telling the story.

'Padman' isn't so bad, though I wish I had a better nickname. But none of this matters, because this story is not about me. It's about how Squidge Dibley peered in the window and destroyed the school.

That's him again. --->

So, now that that's out of the way, here's how everything began, before the beginning.

CHAPTER 2

Our class – 6PU – is pretty bad. We don't *mean* to be bad. Individually, we're all pretty good kids. But sometimes when a school puts a particular combination of kids together in the same class, the mixture just doesn't work.

It's like ice cream and chicken drumsticks. On their own, perfectly fine. But mixed together, a total disaster.

Or like pepperoni and banana. Fine on their own, but put them together on a pizza, and things get disgusting.

Our class – 6PU – is kind of like pepperoni and banana pizza.

STUDENT CASE FILES

The Pritchard Twins: Ainsley and Audrey

- Nobody knows who is who. (Not even their parents.)
- Serial pranksters.
  *See pages 14 and 15
- Holders of the combined Craglands South Primary record for most detentions.

Daniel Kwon-Yoon

- Seventy-three skateboards confiscated since Kindergarten.
- One hundred and forty-two warnings for reckless skateboard riding at school.
- Fourteen broken arms in six years.

Nathan Kobeissi

- Can't stop eating paint.
- Suspended four times for eating wet paintings from the Kindergarten classrooms.

Shane Sloosman

- Born with adult teeth.
- Cuts his own hair due to fear of barbers.

Rebecca Peterson

- Musical genius.
- Sings her answer when asked a question.
- Suspended in Year 5 for 'inappropriate blasting of trumpet during visit by local mayor'.

Lenny Battisto

- Curly haired since birth.
- Once got his finger stuck in Shane's nose, but denied putting it there.

Leanna Kingsley

- Space nut. Obsessed with the solar system.
- Accused Year 1 teacher of being extra-terrestrial. And Year 2 teacher. And Years 3, 4 and 5 teachers.

Abigail Takani

- Collects sugar sachets. (Has nine hundred in her collection.)
- Junior street dancing champion. (Specialist in popping and locking.)

Rennie Grosse

- Once brought a carton of eggs into class. Turned out to be python eggs. School evacuated due to baby python outbreak.
- Obsessed with snakes. Scared of everything else.

That's not even half the class, but you get the idea of how we are the worst ever Year 6 class at Craglands South Primary.

That's why we've had four teachers already, and it's only second term.

Our first teacher was Mr Wirthness.

Well, I say first teacher, but I guess what I really mean is first victim.

CHAPTER 3

(144 days before Squidge Dibley)

Poor Mr Wirthness. He was nervous from day one. Every time someone asked a question, he would jump in fright.

Can I please go to the—

AAAUGH!

Things got out of hand quickly thanks to the Pritchard Twins.

First, they began swapping seats every time he turned his back.

Then they replaced all his whiteboard markers with permanent ones and 'accidentally' hid six live slugs in his coffee mug.

The Pritchard Twins can't help themselves. They've been professional pranksters since they were toddlers. It started when they would blame each other for pooping in the bath.

AUDREY DID POOPIES !!!

Maybe if Mr Wirthness had punished them at the beginning, *the blue-paint incident* wouldn't have happened.

CHAPTER 4

THE BLUE-PAINT INCIDENT
Starring NATHAN KOBEISSI
(121 days before Squidge Dibley)

Nathan Kobeissi has been a paint eater ever since Kindergarten. He's addicted to it like some kids are addicted to sour lollies. **Everyone** knows that you have to keep the paint **LOCKED UP** if Nathan is in the classroom.

STAFF NOTICES

PLEASE REMOVE MOULDY LUNCHES FROM THE FRIDGE
That means YOU, Mr. P.

Who Took my coffee mug?! Please return it to

Do **NOT** Ever let NATHAN K. near the PAINT !!!

FOR SALE! TOYOTA COROLLA 1987 MODEL ONLY 385,900km SEE MR.B

PLEASE STOP PARKING IN MY CAR SPACE! I KNOW WHO YOU ARE!!

REMINDER! School Photo Day Next month! ALL male staff to wear Long trousers.

VOTE NOW for the Staff CHRISTMAS PARTY THEME
1. 'Disco' Fever
2. 'Ship Wrecked
3. Ye Old West

But someone must have forgotten to tell Mr Wirthness. He left *three huge bottles* of ocean-blue watercolour on the bench so we could start painting our Under the Sea mural after recess.

The Pritchard Twins 'accidentally' told Nathan it was there.

PSSST!

He drank all three bottles before recess was over. Sixteen minutes later, his skin started turning blue.

Everyone thought he looked <u>wicked</u>, like a smurf on steroids, but his parents really let Mr Wirthness have it.

Apparently Nathan's poos were blue for two weeks.

CHAPTER 5

(104 days before Squidge Dibley)

Mr Wirthness's problems might have ended there if Crichton Peel hadn't blamed the Pritchard Twins for an <u>EXTRA-STINKY silent fart</u> he did during geography.

THEY DID IT !!!

FIVE REASONS WHY CRICHTON PEEL IS THE MOST ANNOYING HUMAN BEING ON THE PLANET

 BRAGS ABOUT BEING SMARTER THAN EVERYONE ELSE. (HE'S <u>NOT</u>.)

 LOVES GETTING OTHER PEOPLE IN TROUBLE. (ALL THE TIME.)

 THINKS HE'S AN EXPERT ON EVERYTHING. (HE'S <u>NOT</u>.)

 FARTS SILENTLY IN CLASS, THEN BLAMES THE PERSON NEXT TO HIM. (IT'S ALWAYS HIM.)

 KEEPS BITS OF DRIED SNOT UNDER HIS FINGERNAILS IN CASE HE GETS HUNGRY. (HE CHEWS THEM NONSTOP.)

Everybody knew he was lying about the fart. The smell was *vintage Crichton*, but Mr Wirthness sent both twins out of the room.

They got their revenge the same day, with a prank that became known as:

OPERATION SUPERGLUED BUTT CHEEKS
Starring CRICHTON PEEL, the most annoying kid ever

While Ms Bromley, the school maintenance lady, was sawing the chair off Crichton's butt with an angle grinder, Mr Wirthness was called to a meeting with the principal.

He never came back.

CHAPTER 6

Our next teacher, Mr Horkland seemed like he was going to be all right, even though he smelled like my mum's spice rack and talked like a blender full of pebbles.

The problem was that Mr Horkland didn't teach us anything. He never even opened a textbook. Most days he would just make us watch old black-and-white war movies, or show us his collection of model planes.

The whole thing was strange, but we figured it was better than doing regular schoolwork, so we just went along with it.

Once he spent a whole day teaching us to play the mouth trumpet, which is when you puff out your cheeks and hum loudly with your mouth closed.

If you do it right, you actually sound like a real trumpet. Do it wrong and you just sound like you're farting.

Rebecca Peterson totally nailed it. She was louder than anyone else and got every note right. Rebecca is a genius musician. She's been playing nine different instruments since she was three and is pretty much the whole school orchestra.

Mr Horkland was so impressed, he got everyone to stand up and salute while Rebecca stood on his desk and performed *The Last Post*, which is a sad song that armies play on a bugle when a soldier dies.

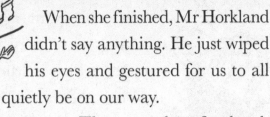

When she finished, Mr Horkland didn't say anything. He just wiped his eyes and gestured for us to all quietly be on our way.

Then, one day after lunch while he was acting out what it was like to fly a German Messerschmitt, Mr Horkland suddenly slumped backwards on the carpet.

It took us ten minutes to realise that it wasn't part of the re-enactment.

It was pretty awkward. None of us knew what to do. So, Rebecca Peterson mouth trumpeted *The Last Post* while we silently saluted him.

CHAPTER 7

(93 days before Squidge Dibley)

Our next teacher was Ms Trigley.

When she first walked in, nobody believed she was a teacher. She looked like the lead singer of a punk-rock band. Half her head was shaved, her fingernails were painted black and she had about a hundred safety pins in her ears.

The first thing she said to us was, 'Rumour has it, you're a bunch of nutjobs.'

She was actually an awesome teacher. Like, she seemed to have a clue about how to fix all the problems with 6PU.

She padlocked the paint cupboard so Nathan couldn't get near it. Then she rearranged all our tables into a spiral and taught every lesson from a different side of the room. I scored a desk right next to the back window, furthest from Crichton who was by the door.

YES!

When the Pritchard Twins put a fake rat on her chair she just picked it up and started stroking it like a cat, without even stopping the lesson.

It turns out that when she was a teenager she had four pet rats named Matty, Patty, Fatty and Rachel.

She told us that they used to sleep in her bed with her. Nobody believed her, so she brought in a photo the next day.

The Pritchard Twins totally worshipped her after that.

When she noticed that the class fish bowl was empty, she brought in her pet puffer fish. That's how we got our class mascot, Bubble O'Gill.

Everyone thought he was excellent.

Except Crichton Peel. Probably because Bubble O'Gill would puff up every time Crichton looked at him.

Anyway, Ms Trigley was pretty much the most *epic teacher* any of us had ever had, and it wasn't long before we all stopped mucking around, especially after Daniel Kwon-Yoon spotted this tattoo in Ms Trigley's armpit:

She looked like she could do it, too.

And best of all, she seemed to find Crichton Peel as annoying as we did.

When he dobbed on Leanna Kingsley for talking in class, Ms Trigley leaned in really close to him and yelled,

'SNITCHES GET STITCHES!'

For a while, school was okay and it looked like we might actually learn something after all without anyone getting maimed. But like I've said, sometimes when you mix a bunch of kids together who shouldn't be mixed together, it's only a matter of time before something goes wrong. Even with a teacher as boss as Ms Trigley.

CHAPTER 8

(80 days before Squidge Dibley)

The funny thing about being a narrator is that I can see now where the story began to go wrong. It's kind of like having a superpower that you can't use, because the story is going to happen no matter what you do about it. All you can do is keep telling the story.

Everything fell apart when Ms Trigley found out that the thing that scared us the most was public speaking.

She said that it was crazy to be scared of public speaking, because everyone knows that the only thing that anyone should be scared of is a Zombie Shark Clown.

She told us we were going to have a Speech Slam.

It sounded dangerous, but she explained that a Speech Slam is just a cool name for a public-speaking competition.

We had two days to prepare and these were the rules:

Bring in something
cool, freaky or unusual
from home.
Give a five-minute speech
about it.
BEST SPEECH WINS A PRIZE

Straightaway, Crichton Peel started bragging that he was going to win the prize and nobody else should even bother trying.

It was game on.

Looking back on the whole disaster, it's easy to see the crux of the problem: Ms Trigley should have been clearer about what she meant by 'cool, freaky or unusual'.

The day before the Speech Slam, Ms Trigley was away sick and our substitute was our PE teacher, Mr Potshut.

Mr Potshut is so HUGE he has to turn sideways to walk through the door, and he has no idea about anything other than sports.

Everyone kept asking him whether it would be okay to bring random, crazy stuff to school for the Speech Slam.

We had to explain to him six times what a Speech Slam was, but he still didn't get it. In the end he told everyone: 'Just use your brain.'

This is exactly the kind of useless answer that is not good to say to a class of kids who had been churning through teachers like most classes churn through glue sticks.

On the day of the Speech Slam, Ms Trigley was late to school. Maybe if she had been on time, she might have been able to stop us bringing all our 'cool, freaky and unusual' stuff into the school.

But she wasn't.

So, she didn't.

CHAPTER 9

By the time Ms Trigley arrived, the classroom was a full-scale catastrophe.

Three desks had been sawn in half. The carpet had been mowed. Shane Sloosman had been stung on his left leg by Daniel Kwon-Yoon's pet scorpion and he had Rennie Grosse's pet python wrapped around his right leg. The whole classroom was covered in a layer of the Pritchard Twins' atomic-strength Swedish itching powder. Lenny Battisto had Rebecca Peterson's grandmother's false teeth stuck in his mouth. Abigail Takani's ponytail had been nail-gunned to the door. And a swarm of wasps was chasing everyone around the room.

In the middle of it all, Crichton Peel was standing on his desk screeching that his monkey-claw backscratcher was better than anything else anybody had brought in. (It seriously wasn't. It was made of plastic.) Nobody had even noticed that Rennie Grosse's pet python had swallowed somebody's poodle.

Ms Trigley just looked kind of green in the face, which was unusual for her. She tried to get everything under control, but then she accidentally stepped in the bear trap that Shane Sloosman had left on the floor and caught an unexploded, vintage, Russian hand grenade that someone had just lobbed through the air.

The whole school was put into lockdown and Miss Trigley had to be rushed away in an ambulance, with the bear trap still clamped around her ankle.

Maybe things would have been different if Squidge Dibley had arrived earlier. It's impossible to say. It was still seventy-seven days before he would appear at the back window; the same window from which we watched the ambulance take Ms Trigley away.

'I'm going to miss Ms Trigley,' said Abigail Takani, gulping down five sachets of sugar. 'I hope she comes back soon.'

'SHE WON'T BE COMING BACK IN A HURRY!' boomed a voice from behind us.

Everyone jumped in shock. 'Uh-oh,' muttered Abigail, swallowing another sachet of sugar.

The school principal was standing in the doorway.

CHAPTER 10

Her name is Principal Shoutmouth.

Shoutmouth isn't her real surname. It's Schlouwdtnmirth, but nobody can pronounce it.

Can I please have a raise, Principal ... um ... Shloopymoth ... I mean ... Shnorgenmoof ... ... err ... Shumpymunf ... um ... never mind.

And she does shout A LOT. Like, A LOT. None of us can understand how someone so small can be so LOUD.

Anyway, Principal Shoutmouth walked in, and everyone FREAKED OUT. First, because there were still stray wasps buzzing around the room, but also because Principal Shoutmouth never leaves her office. (She has her own private bathroom that nobody else is allowed to use, not even the other teachers.) She's like an ominous force that looms over the whole school, even though she's the same height as the smallest Kindergarten kid.

She shouted at us all to BE QUIET.

Then she explained that Ms Trigley was going on a special holiday called 'indefinite leave'. Lenny Battisto asked how Ms Trigley could be on holidays when she had only just left and wouldn't have even had time to book any plane tickets or anything, and anyway how would she get through the metal detectors at the airport with a bear trap stuck to her leg and –

Principal Shoutmouth told him to **ZIP HIS TALK HOLE**.

Then she told us that it was **UNACCEPTABLE** for us to keep changing teachers as often as we changed our socks.

'But I never change my socks,' said Shane Sloosman.

'That explains the stink,' said the Pritchard Twins.

Principal Shoutmouth shouted, **'LATCH UP YOUR LIPS!'**

Then she explained that the teachers' union had banned any more teachers coming to Craglands South Primary, so Ms Trigley's replacement was going to be someone from the school.

'I feel sick!' cried Shane Sloosman.

We all did. But things were about to get a whole lot worse.

CHAPTER 11

Everyone went crazy trying to guess who our new teacher would be.

SUSPECT 1

Mr Potshut

* PE teacher.
* Cuts hair with sheep shears.
* Cro-Magnon-like forehead.
* Permanent confused look.
* Body wider than door.
* Likes running after balls.
* Brain might be partially canine.

SUSPECT 2

Mrs Yilmaz

* Volunteer ethics teacher.
* Smiles non-stop. (Enormous teeth.)
* Brings in delicious, home-made Turkish delight.
* Speaks like a dictionary.
* Probably too smart to endure more than an hour a week teaching us.

SUSPECT 3

Ms Sloane

* Librarian.
* Permanent angry face.
* Obsessed with silence.
* Never laughs.
* Clothes always covered in dog fur.
* Hates books with pictures.
* Wanted to be a famous actress; once starred in a pet-food commercial.

SUSPECT 4

Ms Bromley

* School maintenance lady.
* SPECIAL SKILLS:
  - Extreme leaf-blowing.
  - High-speed lawn mowing.
  - Possum hunting. Has been trying for two years to capture the possums that steal packets of chips from the canteen.

Everyone was yelling over the top of each other until Principal Shoutmouth shouted, **'SHUT YOUR TALK TRAPS!'**

Then, she told us who our new teacher was going to be.

CHAPTER 12

Everyone froze as we watched her say the name. Since I'm the narrator, I need to tell you to read the name out loud in super-slow motion, because that's how it sounded to us when Principal Shoutmouth said it.

VICE PRINCIPAL HOOVESLY.

This was BAD NEWS.

BAD NEWS!

Vice Principal Hoovesly is THE WORST!

THE. WORST.

Just thinking about him makes my mouth taste like six flavours of vomit.

parmesan cheese and apple juice

Fish and ice-cream

carrot and yoghurt

broccoli and custard

beef and pineapple

sausage and milk

If I had to write a fifty-page essay on all the reasons why Vice Principal Hoovesly is **THE WORST**, I'd run out of paper before I even got started.

Here are the top eight (from a list that could easily reach eight hundred).

HE HATES KIDS. I swear he wishes that schools didn't have kids in them. He spends all his time finding reasons to give out detentions. Or worse. Which leads me to my next point.

HIS PUNISHMENTS ARE EVIL. Once, he caught Abigail Takani putting a rotten banana in the bin. It was fully black and mushy. But he made her take it out of the bin and then **EAT IT IN FRONT OF THE WHOLE SCHOOL AT ASSEMBLY!** And the banana wasn't even **HERS!** She'd found it on the ground and was trying to do a good thing by cleaning it up. See: evil.

HE NEVER FORGETS ANYTHING YOU'VE DONE WRONG. EVER. Once I was late to school because my dad slept in. Ever since then, every time Vice Principal Hoovesly sees me he says, 'Glad to see you're not late today, Padman O'Donnell.' Except that it happened **FIVE YEARS AGO! I WAS IN YEAR 1!** But he still says it **ALL THE TIME!**

HE NEVER SMILES. His face is frozen in a permanent scowl like he just ate a cracker smeared with fresh dog poop.

HE CONFISCATES EVERYTHING. Seriously, if he finds anything that's not officially permitted at school, he takes it. And guess who decides what's permitted? He does! Daniel Kwon-Yoon has had seventy-three skateboards confiscated. Daniel rides a skateboard to school – which is permitted – but he always forgets to put it in his bag, so Vice Principal Hoovesly just takes them and **NEVER GIVES THEM BACK!**

HE WEARS GIANT SUNGLASSES ALL THE TIME – even when he's inside – so you never know where he's looking. A lot of people believe that he has no eyeballs.

HE SMELLS LIKE CABBAGE BOILED IN AFTERSHAVE. And not nice aftershave either, but that nasty stuff they sell for three dollars at discount shops right before Father's Day.

HE SPITS WHEN HE TALKS. It's like he has a fire hose at the back of his throat.

Okay, so all of that is **BAD**, right? But none of those is the weirdest part. Or the worst.

CHAPTER 13

Once in Year 2 I had to take a permission note to the office for an excursion to the zoo. When I walked in I could hear this motorised grinding sound. Then I saw Vice Principal Hoovesly SHARPENING HIS FINGERNAILS WITH AN ELECTRIC PENCIL SHARPENER!

He didn't see me, but I was too shocked to say anything, so I just stood there watching. As he finished each fingernail, he filed the edges with sandpaper.

Then – I kid you not – he took off his shoes and socks and SHARPENED HIS TOENAILS TOO! They were all long and skinny like eagle claws. It was DISGUSTING!!!

46

As far as I was concerned, nothing I was going to see at the zoo could be freakier than what I had just witnessed, so I backed out of the office and ran.

Vice Principal Hoovesly's talons are one of the first things you hear about when you start at Craglands South Primary. They're a Craglands legend.

Over the years, there have been thousands of theories about why he keeps his fingernails so long and sharp:

He hunts rats at night.   He's half vulture.

He's a vampire. Or a werewolf.
Or a werepire. Or a vampwolf.

Vice Principal Hoovesly normally never teaches classes – at least he hasn't for the entire time I've been at Craglands South. I heard that he's not allowed to because once he drop-kicked a kid out a window.

Leanna Kingsley says that she has actually seen the kid he did it to. She says that the kid is grown up now but he still has a dent in his skull and a double limp from breaking both his ankles when he landed.

But then again, Leanna Kingsley also says that her dad works for NASA and that he lets her play in NASA's zero-gravity room, so she's not really a reliable source.

Ol' Hoovesly done this to me when I was a wee lad!

Anyway, when we heard that Vice Principal Hoovesly was our new teacher we were all horrified. I'd sooner be taught by a plastic bag full of camel dung if I had the choice. It would definitely smell better.

If only Ms Trigley hadn't given us the Speech Slam assignment. Or Mr Horkland had survived his re-enactment of the Battle of Britain. Or Mr Wirthness had been more … well, actually I don't think he was ever going to make it at Craglands. I heard he's training to be a pet therapist now.

OHMMM …

As soon as Principal Shoutmouth left the class-room, Vice Principal Hoovesly appeared in the doorway and just stood there staring at us.

Then he walked slowly around the room, chuckling to himself, his weird cabbage-boiled-in-aftershave smell wafting up our nostrils.

Things got bad, fast.

CHAPTER 14

First, Vice Principal Hoovesly made Crichton Peel his special assistant.

Then he rearranged all our desks back into boring rows. Luckily, I kept my spot at the back by the window.

Next, he confiscated everything we'd brought in for the Speech Slam. He made us carry it all to his office 'for safekeeping'. He said we would get everything back *if and when* we proved that we were well behaved.

Luckily I'd forgotten to bring anything, especially since I'd been planning to bring my dad's mummified cat.

Dad had found it buried in the soggy bog swamp in the corner of our backyard.

It looked like a cat-shaped piece of beef jerky and was THE FREAKIEST THING I'D EVER SEEN. Dad reckoned that it could have been about ten thousand years old and that it had been perfectly preserved in the bog, like those human–Hobbit Neanderthal fossils that archaeologists believe could be the missing link between monkeys and humans.

Dad was so excited when we found it, he took it straight to Craglands Museum to see if they could carbon date it for him to find out how old it was. But the attendant at the front desk pointed out that the cat was wearing a plastic collar with a phone number engraved on the tag.

Dad hadn't noticed it because it was all caked in mud.

When we got home, we called the number. A second later we heard the phone ring next door at our neighbours', the Blentons, house.

Then we remembered how their cat went missing two years earlier.

It was right around the time our sewerage pipes broke and our backyard flooded with poop.

Apricot always used to do his business in our back corner, so I guess he must have got trapped when the poo volcano erupted from under the lawn.

Mum insisted that Dad give Apricot back to the Blentons. But Dad said that would be cruel since he looked more like a dried apricot now and besides, they'd had a new cat for ages.

So, Mum told Dad to 'just get rid of it', though I don't think she meant for him to cover it in cling wrap and hide it in a Tupperware container under the house, which is what Dad did. He explained to me that sometimes Mum didn't have the same eye for a rare collectable specimen that he did and that when you find something unique, you should hold on to it.

I was going to ask him if that's why Mum married him, but I was keen to get out from under the house by that point.

APRICOT II

CHAPTER 15

It was just as well I didn't bring the mummy cat in for the Speech Slam, because Vice Principal Hoovesly **hates** pets. He hates them almost as much as the school maintenance lady, Ms Bromley, hates possums. And she hates possums almost as much as Vice Principal Hoovesly hates kids.

Anyway, when Vice Principal Hoovesly noticed Daniel Kwon-Yoon's pet scorpion climbing up the wall, he STABBED IT WITH A FINGERNAIL!

We were still in shock when he picked up Rennie Grosse's pet python and flung it out the front window, poodle and all.

'My snake!!!' screamed Rennie.

He started crying, like, LOUDLY. Vice Principal Hoovesly wrote on the whiteboard:

CLASSROOM RULES

No crying.

Then he gave Rennie a detention note!

Abigail Takani handed Rennie a tissue so Rennie could blow his nose. But then Vice Principal Hoovesly wrote on the board:

No sharing tissues.

Then he gave Abigail a detention note and said, 'And I hope you're not still throwing out perfectly good bananas, Miss Takani.'

Like I've said, he NEVER FORGETS ANYTHING! Daniel Kwon-Yoon whispered angrily, 'That's messed up, man.'

Then Vice Principal Hoovesly wrote:

No talking.

And he gave Daniel a detention too!

It was deadly silent around the classroom now.

The only sound was Shane Sloosman feverishly scratching the big swollen lump on his leg where he had been stung by Daniel's now-dead scorpion.

Then Vice Principal Hoovesly wrote:

No scratching.

Detention for Shane!

But Vice Principal Hoovesly just kept writing more rules.

No blinking.

'No blinking?!' shouted Lenny Battisto, blinking.

Vice Principal Hoovesly added:

No shouting.

Two detentions for Lenny.

The rest of the day was torture, especially for Shane, who was turning yellow from the scorpion venom.

When he begged to go to the school nurse, Vice Principal Hoovesly told him that he should have thought of the consequences before he let the scorpion sting him.

And when Shane tried to explain that he hadn't let it, Vice Principal Hoovesly gave him a detention for lying, because if he hadn't let it sting him, he wouldn't be suffering from scorpion poisoning.

Things kept getting worse.

More rules were written on the board.

No loud breathing or coughing.

No breaking wind.

No talking without raising your hand.

No raising of hands.

We knew things were going to be GRIM, but this was a new level of GRIM. It was OFF-THE-SCALE GRIM.

GRIM-O-METER

Vice Principal Hoovesly got Crichton Peel to hand out a surprise maths test, full of questions about stuff we hadn't even learned yet, and while we were doing the test he carved his name into the classroom door with his fingernails. It was actually pretty nicely carved, but that doesn't change the fact that IT WAS DISGUSTING!

Then – and this is the worst bit – he got Crichton Peel to take the batteries out of the classroom clock. And he banned people wearing watches in class.

Now we would never have any idea how long we had until the end of the day.

WHAT SORT OF MONSTER WOULD DO THAT?!

The reign of Vice Principal Hoovesly had begun.

CHAPTER 16

(64 days before Squidge Dibley)

I wish I could say that things lightened up, but as I've said before, I'm just the narrator, so I can only tell the story exactly as it happened. And in the weeks that followed, the classroom became like a graveyard. Nobody smiled. Nobody spoke. Nobody blinked. We were all too scared.

Only Crichton Peel was enjoying himself. Vice Principal Hoovesly put him in charge whenever he was away supervising Swim Squad training with the other classes.

Vice Principal Hoovesly is OBSESSED with Swim Squad. It used to be voluntary, but Vice Principal Hoovesly made it compulsory for every student at Craglands South Primary, whether they knew how to swim or not.

He is desperate to win the **ANNUAL JUNIOR REGIONAL WATER WAR.** It's a yearly swimming carnival between Craglands South Primary and Craglands North Private, which is this posh school where all the kids from rich families go.

They have this amazing, Olympic-sized swimming pool with crystal-clear water. Their swim team all look like human dolphins.

We've never won against them, ever. In fact, we have never won against ANYBODY.

There is a rumour that Vice Principal Hoovesly thinks that Craglands North Private will give him a job as their swim coach if we ever beat them.

When anyone complains about squad training, he yells, **'EVERYONE SWIMS 'TIL CRAGLANDS SOUTH WINS.'**

So, every class has to do an hour of swimming training every week, **EVEN IN WINTER!** Even the Kindergarten kids!

It's not fun swimming, either. Just **laps** back and forth, with no free time afterwards. And if anyone stops swimming, he makes the whole class do an extra lap.

The worst thing is that we have to train in the pool at the senior citizens home across the road from the school. The water is warm and yellow, and there is always something disgusting

floating in it, like tufts of hair and Band-Aids with bits of scab stuck to them.

Once, there was an oversized nappy with brown ooze leaking out of it. Another time there was a big dark lump on the bottom of the pool. Shane Sloosman swam down to check it out and it turned out to be a dead rat.

Worst of all was the time we were practising laps of butterfly and something soft and green bumped into Lenny Battisto's goggles. He flicked it away, but Rennie Grosse was surging up out of the water behind him with his mouth open, and the green thing went RIGHT INTO HIS MOUTH.

And it was a *toe!*

An actual, real-life, rotten human toe!

It had fallen off an old guy who had been doing aqua aerobics.

Straightaway, Rennie started throwing up right there in the water. And everyone who was swimming in the lane behind him started SWALLOWING ALL HIS VOMIT, and then they all started throwing up as well.

The whole lane turned into a churning barf fountain.

And meanwhile the toe kept on bobbing around and bumping against people's faces. Everyone was screaming and vomiting and trying not to let the toe touch them, or swallow other people's vomit.

It was horrible.

Then Vice Principal Hoovesly started yelling at everyone to keep swimming, and when we tried to explain that there was a rotten toe and a whole heap of upchuck in the water, he shouted, 'STOP BEING SO CHILDISH!'

So, we had to keep swimming.

But this was nothing compared to the disgustingness that lay ahead.

CHAPTER 17

We very quickly learned that Crichton Peel couldn't be trusted when Vice Principal Hoovesly left him in charge. The power totally went to his head.

DETENTION
Daniel K.-Y. x 5
Leanna K. x 4
Ainsley P. x 10
Audrey P. x 10
Padman O'D. x 3
Nathan K. x 2
Rebecca P. x 1
Abigail T. x 1
Lenny B. x 8
Shane S. x 9
Rennie G. x4

These were dark days. Everyone was twitchy. Nathan Kobeissi spent most lunchtimes licking paint off the school mural.

Rebecca Peterson stopped practising her trumpet (her real one, not the mouth trumpet, though she stopped practising that too). Shane Sloosman's face got a weird stress rash and his eyebrows grew bushy.

The Pritchard Twins stopped trying any pranks. Even Bubble O'Gill looked depressed.

I thought about complaining to my mum and dad, but they had their own problems. My dad had quit his job as a nurse to pursue his dream of being an entrepreneur.

I'd asked Dad what that was, and he said that it was someone who doesn't have to 'answer to the man', which was a weird thing to say, because Dad's boss at the hospital where he worked was a nice lady who used to let me eat the cookies from the staff kitchen whenever we visited.

Mum, who has never missed a day of work in her life, said that an entrepreneur is another word for a lazy bum, but she agreed that Dad could take six months to try it out, on the condition that he stopped sleeping in all the time and that he did the housework.

Ever since then Dad had been dreaming up a bunch of different business ideas.

None of them had worked so far, plus the house had been getting pretty messy. Things between Mum and Dad got kind of tense, so I figured that telling them that my teacher was a psycho-weirdo with raptor claws probably wouldn't help the situation.

Besides, Vice Principal Hoovesly never wrote anything nasty on any of our schoolwork, so there was no hard evidence of how truly evil he was.

We thought about telling other teachers about what he was up to, but they never would have believed us. It would be his word against ours. And nobody was brave enough to visit Principal Shoutmouth's office.

So, we soon started to spend our lunchtimes hatching plans to take Vice Principal Hoovesly down.

CHAPTER 18

We came up with some good ideas.

OPERATION: GET HOOVESLY

But Vice Principal Hoovesly must have known we were up to something, or maybe Crichton ratted on us, because one day Hoovesly announced that we were going to spend the rest of the week working on a special art project.

He called it:

THE HOOVESLY
PORTRAIT
PRIZE

This was the project:

   * Create a portrait or sculpture of
your teacher (Vice Principal Hoovesly).
      * Use only bright colours.

The whole project seemed suspicious, but
it was a break from the non-stop maths we'd
been doing all week. Besides, Vice Principal
Hoovesly said that the five best artworks
would be awarded homework immunity

vouchers that could be used at any time, and that the student who created the best-judged artwork would win an **UNLIMITED CANTEEN VOUCHER!**

Everyone went crazy for it. The competition was even fiercer than for the Speech Slam.

We spent three days working on our portraits. Some of them were not good.

But there are some solid artists in our class.

Leanna Kingsley brought in a huge supply of professional paints, and Nathan Kobeissi brought in a wheelbarrow load of modelling clay so he could sculpt a Vice Principal Hoovesly statue. (Nathan wasn't allowed near the paint.)

For the first time any of us could remember, school was actually almost fun. Once, I even noticed Vice Principal Hoovesly smile while he was posing, though I couldn't be sure.

Everyone desperately wanted to win. Especially me. I needed that canteen voucher badly – for reasons I'll explain in a moment.

But it isn't easy to make a great portrait of someone as disgusting as Vice Principal Hoovesly, so my first attempts didn't turn out so good.

I finally got it looking pretty awesome and everyone was sure I was going to win.

by
PADMAN

At the end of the third day, we put all the portraits on display around the classroom. Leanna Kingsley's mum donated a bunch of fancy frames, which made the portraits seem like they should have been hung in an art gallery.

Vice Principal Hoovesly took ages to judge them all. He shuffled around the room in what seemed like slow motion, peering at each artwork so closely that his nose almost pressed against them. It was *so tense*. The only sounds in the room were Shane Sloosman's nervously chattering teeth and the eerie squeaking of Vice Principal Hoovesly's leather shoes. Everyone wanted the prize.

Finally, after he'd kept us waiting for over an hour, he told us he would announce the winners at a special ceremony.

When we asked when, he smirked and said: 'All in good time.'

I smelled a rat. And I was pretty sure it wasn't the possums that were living in the school's roof.

YOU DIDN'T SEE ME

CHAPTER 19

Weeks passed. None of us knew it, but we were creeping closer and closer to Squidge Dibley's arrival.

All the while, Vice Principal Hoovesly still hadn't announced the winners of the portrait competition. It was torture for us, but nobody dared misbehave.

Soon the most awkward night of the year came around: parent–teacher interview evening, where parents visit the classroom and hear how their kids are going.

We'd all been hoping that when our parents met Vice Principal Hoovesly in person, they'd realise how disgustingly evil he was. But he hid his list of rules, and when each parent arrived he gave them a tour of the portraits.

All the parents loved him, even though he told them that we should all be doing at least two hours of study every night to help us get ready for high school.

My mum and dad said afterwards that they thought he was the best teacher I'd ever had, and that they could tell how much we all loved Vice Principal Hoovesly from how much work we'd put into our portraits.

I mean, how can adults be so dumb?!

The next day, Vice Principal Hoovesly announced that it was time for the special ceremony.

It was so quiet, you could hear an ant fart.

Then, he said that there was one clear winner.

Everyone looked at me. Daniel Kwon-Yoon gave me the thumbs-up.

'The winner …' said Vice Principal Hoovesly, taking his time. 'Of the first ever Hoovesly Portrait Prize is …'

I closed my eyes.

'CRICHTON PEEL.'

'Now *that*,' said Vice Principal Hoovesly, 'is a work of art.'

We couldn't believe it.

Then Vice Principal Hoovesly said that Crichton's portrait was so good, he was awarding him ALL the prizes.

Daniel Kwon-Yoon asked Vice Principal Hoovesly if he was going to take all the other portraits down if they were all so bad. Vice Principal Hoovesly gave him a detention on the spot for talking in class. And then he confiscated

Daniel's skateboard just to show that he could.

The portraits stayed.

We'd been played, big time. So had our parents.

The list of rules reappeared, printed in huge letters on a board at the front of the room. Only, now he had added a bunch of new ones, like:

No unnecessary movement.
No smiling.
Look straight ahead at all times.

The last one was almost impossible for me with my desk right next to the back window.

Even though I could only see a bit of the roof of the library and the occasional cloud, anything was better than staring at Vice Principal Hoovesly's skull-dome.

So, I was lucky that he was busy writing on the whiteboard when the day finally arrived. The day Squidge Dibley appeared at the window.

CHAPTER 20

(THE DAY OF DIBLEY)

Nobody else saw him except me and Bubble O'Gill.

I didn't know it was Squidge Dibley then. Like I've said before, all I knew was that it was impossible for **anyone** to be at that window unless they were standing on a ladder, or hanging from a helicopter or were some sort of half-spider creature.

Squidge pressed his face against the glass and smiled at me, like it was a perfectly normal thing for someone to peer through a third-storey window.

I was so stunned that I instantly broke rules five, six and seven.

No blinking.

No shouting

No coughing.

In the split-second before Vice Principal Hoovesly spun around to see what the commotion was, Squidge Dibley disappeared.

Now Vice Principal Hoovesly was staring at me with the same expression that a killer cobra gives a mouse that has just wandered into its nest.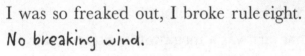

I was so freaked out, I broke rule eight.

No breaking wind.

And I broke it, like, *super loudly.*

Desks rattled. Dust shook from the ceilings of the classrooms beneath ours. I heard possums scatter in the roof.

I'd dropped one *seriously toxic stink*.

Before Vice Principal Hoovesly could do anything, Crichton Peel yelled:

'PONG!!!'

I can't blame Crichton.

That fart was a mega-tonne nostril nuke.

On the super-septic-stinkiness scale, it was off the charts.

FART-O-METER

CHAPTER 21

My monster fart was my dad's fault.

He was halfway through his six-month experiment as an entrepreneur/lazy bum and so far none of his business ideas had taken off.

PRAM-MOWER 3000

PUPPY JETPACK

BOG BIKE

Then one day he found an **enormous** electric cooker and an **industrial-sized** walk-in freezer at the junkyard across the road from our house.

Yes, we live across the road from a junkyard. Dad spends a lot of time there looking for stuff that he can recycle into something that will make us rich. Mum banned him from going there, but he sneaks over when she's at work.

Anyway, when Dad saw the giant electric cooker and industrial freezer at the junkyard, he got in one of his **excited** moods and bought them both straightaway. As he was dragging them across the road to our house, he noticed a rusty old postal scooter and he bought that as well.

Mum wasn't happy, but Dad insisted that this idea was **THE BIG ONE.**

The one that would make us rich.

He said he was going to start a home-cooked, hot-curry delivery business.

He called it **HURRY CURRY.**

Dad wrote his business plan on the garage wall:

THE BIG ONE — BUSINESS PLAN

Cook 10,000 serves of curry.

Freeze curries in industrial freezer.

Deliver curries on (repaired) postal scooter to hungry customers.

Make mega dollars.

NEVER HAVE TO WORK FOR THE MAN AGAIN.

Dad got really into it. First he hand-painted a huge sign and put it up in the front yard.

Then he bought hundreds of kilos of curry ingredients and started cooking around the clock. Unfortunately, the only room in the house that could fit the jumbo cooker was the bathroom.

When the delicious curry aromas mixed with the not-so-delicious bathroom odours, it created a seriously unearthly stench. Our neighbours, the Blentons, kept knocking on our front door asking if our sewerage pipes were broken again.

It was all going okay until the morning I got out of bed and the floor was hot and squelchy and kind of spicy. Turns out that the electric cooker had a leak in it. That's the thing about junkyards: all the stuff there is junk.

But now a huge river of spicy pork curry was flooding down the hallway, all the way out the back door and into the Blentons' yard.

Dad tried to soak it all up with naan bread, but it was no use. We had to rip up all the carpet and scrub everything for days.

Dad totally lost interest in HURRY CURRY after that.

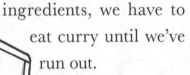

Except that he had already made A LOT of frozen curries.

And because Dad is paying Mum back for the cost of the equipment and all the ingredients, we have to eat curry until we've run out.

Breakfast: curry.
Lunch: curry.
Dinner: curry.
Dessert: curry.
Snacks: curry.

It's not that I don't like Dad's curries. They're fine. Just not for every meal. EVERY DAY!

By my calculations, I'll be graduating from high school by the time we've eaten them all.

The taste is okay. Dad actually made some good flavours. It's the aftermath that is the problem (and the reason why I needed to win Hoovesly's canteen voucher). My butt gets transformed into a gas bazooka.

Usually I hold all the curry farts in until I get home, and let them all out in one long fart.

The longest so far went for nine seconds and changed octave four times, but at least that had been in the privacy of my bedroom.

There was nothing private about *this* stink symphony.

CHAPTER 22

Anyone else narrating this story might have left the next bit out. But I figure that I need to tell the **whole** truth about what happened.

Because what happened was this:

Squidge Dibley's sudden appearance at the third-storey window made me accidentally detonate the extra-spicy beef-and-dhal curry vapours I'd been holding in since breakfast.

It sounded like a moose playing a tuba.

Things got pretty wild after that.

Everyone ignored Vice Principal Hoovesly's **NO TALKING** rule and started yelling, '*Paaaad*!'

And, 'Oh *man*!'

And, '*Man*, Padman, that *pongs*!'

I was sure Vice Principal Hoovesly was about to drop fifty years' worth of detentions on me. But then his face twisted and he gasped, 'SO ... STINKY!'

Lenny Battisto burst out laughing so hard that he fell backwards and knocked himself out on Abigail Takani's desk.

Now everyone *really LOST it.*

I guess it was only a matter of time before all the pent-up energy that had been building up during Vice Principal Hoovesly's regime came exploding out.

That time was now. The whole class went nuts.

'PADMAN O'DONNELL!!!' yelled Vice Principal Hoovesly over the chaos.

He stomped towards my desk and yelled, spit flying from his lips, 'IF YOUR BOWELS EVER INTERRUPT MY CLASS AGAIN, I WILL PERSONALLY SEE TO IT THAT YOUR BUTTOCKS ARE PERMANENTLY HUNG FROM THE FLAGPOLE!'

I thought about what Vice Principal Hoovesly was suggesting.

But I figured that the likelihood of actually making it happen was pretty low.

For a start, where would he find a doctor to perform a butt removal? And even then, surely a medical procedure like that would need a permission note from my parents, and I couldn't imagine my dad or mum signing something like that. Well, maybe Dad would, but only because he'd be curious to see if it was scientifically possible.

I give permission for my son, Padman O'Donnell, to have his butt surgically removed and put on display on the school flagpole.
Yours sincerely,

A. O'Donnell

CHAPTER 23

'**I WILL NOT BE MADE A FOOL OF!**' yelled Vice Principal Hoovesly, his fingernails digging into my desk.

I could see myself reflected in his glasses, and I looked every bit as freaked out as I felt. I shrank down into my chair.

Vice Principal Hoovesly opened his mouth to speak again, but was interrupted by a faint knock on the door.

'I'm not finished with you yet,' he hissed.

I imagined what would happen when he had finished with me.

HERE LIES
PADMAN O'DONNELL
RESTING IN PIECES
AFTER BEING DROP-KICKED
FROM A THIRD-STOREY WINDOW
FOR UNCORKING A
FORCE 10 FART IN CLASS

Vice Principal Hoovesly stomped impatiently to the door and flung it open, yelling, **'WHAT DO YOU WA—'**

He froze mid-word.

Principal Shoutmouth was standing in the doorway.

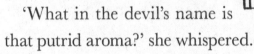

Everyone gasped, including Principal Shoutmouth, who had just smelled the lingering after-tang of my curry-bomb.

'What in the devil's name is that putrid aroma?' she whispered.

'Err …' muttered Vice Principal Hoovesly.

'Err, indeed,' whispered Principal Shoutmouth, clamping her fingers over her nose. 'This classroom smells like rotten dog eggs.'

Vice Principal Hoovesly threw an evil glance at me. I figured that my life only had a few minutes left. Yet, my brain was spiralling in confusion. For a start, why was Principal Shoutmouth whispering? She *always* shouted. **ALWAYS.** Even when she was whispering. But, here she was having a hushed conversation with Vice Principal Hoovesly.

Plus, there were bigger questions bashing about inside my skull.

Who was the kid I'd seen at the window?

Had I really even seen him at all?

Or had I just been hallucinating?

All the answers came at once, because next thing Principal Shoutmouth whispered, '6PU, I'd like you to welcome a new student.'

Shane Sloosman shot up his hand and asked, 'Why are you whispering?'

Principal Shoutmouth said, 'Shhhhh.'

She went on. 'His name is Squidge Dibley.'

CHAPTER 24

Squidge Dibley shuffled in holding a little rectangular briefcase. He was wearing enormous square glasses and his hair looked like some kind of squishy version of the Sydney Opera House. It was the same kid I'd seen at the back window, no question.

Vice Principal Hoovesly tapped his foot impatiently like he couldn't wait for the new kid to sit down and for Principal Shoutmouth to get out.

'Mr Dibley has transferred here from Craglands West Military College,' whispered Principal Shoutmouth.

Military college, I thought.

I'd heard of it, but I didn't know anything about it. I'd always imagined that it must have been some sort of secret training-centre for elite soldiers of the future. But looking at Squidge clutching his little briefcase, he seemed nothing like an elite soldier. But then again, he *had* just peered through a third-storey window. I figured that maybe he'd learnt mad rock-climbing skills at military college and must have sped up the wall while Principal Shoutmouth wasn't looking.

'Now, 6PU,' continued Principal Shoutmouth in a whisper. 'Your class has a reputation for being the quietest and best behaved at Craglands South Primary, thanks to the excellent teaching of Vice Principal Hoovesly.'

We all rolled our eyes.

'Squidge Dibley here is a very special young man.' Her face became even sterner than usual and she looked every one of us in the eye, and said, 'It is most important that this calm and quiet behaviour continues.'

Looking back at everything that has happened since, I understand why Principal Shoutmouth said this. But at the time it just seemed like one of those dumb things that teachers say, like 'Put your listening ears on,' or 'If the wind changes, your face will stay like that.'

Squidge Dibley looked around the room like an astronomer might look around the night sky, while Principal Shoutmouth and Vice Principal Hoovesly had a final whispered conversation.

As soon as Principal Shoutmouth left, Vice Principal Hoovesly glared down at Squidge.

I felt sorry for this strange-looking kid with a name weirder than mine who was being dumped into a class with **the worst teacher on earth**. It was like watching a baby lamb being put into a hyena enclosure. I figured that he wouldn't last the week.

'Sit down, child,' muttered Vice Principal Hoovesly impatiently, pointing to the empty seat next to me. 'And don't expect any special treatment in my classroom.'

Squidge smiled a big, wide, weird smile.

Then he walked to his seat. Only, he didn't exactly walk, he sort of … squidged.

squidge *[verb] walking in a manner in which the arms and legs stretch with each step, causing the person to resemble a human elastic band.*

By the time Squidge arrived at his seat, it looked like his legs had doubled in length.

'Wicked,' whispered the Pritchard Twins.

'Mega-wicked,' added Daniel Kwon-Yoon.

When Squidge climbed up into his chair, he was normal sized again.

Rebecca Peterson whistled in admiration.

Squidge didn't seem to notice the attention. He was busy having a staring competition with Bubble O'Gill.

'What was I saying before we were interrupted?' asked Vice Principal Hoovesly.

Crichton shot up his hand. 'You were telling Padman that you will not be made a fool of.'

I wished that a tiny meteorite could have crashed through the roof and pulverised Crichton for good. But it didn't.

'Correct, Crichton,' said Vice Principal Hoovesly, approvingly.

'In my classroom, flatulence will not be tolerated! We do not behave like incontinent primates.' He slammed his sharpened fingernails into his desk and suddenly shouted, **'ISN'T THAT RIGHT, PADMAN O'DONNELL?!'**

My mouth went dry.

I tried to remember what incontinent meant. It sounded like something to do with geography, but it was also a word that my dad used to explain why Grandpa O'Donnell wears grown-up nappies.

'I SAID, ISN'T THAT RIGHT, PADMAN O'DONNELL?!!!' shouted Vice Principal Hoovesly, even louder.

I forced out a tiny 'Yes', but my voice was so croaky that it sounded like 'Kiss?'.

Shane Sloosman snorted with laughter. Vice Principal Hoovesly flung a dictionary at him, knocking Shane off his chair.

'BECAUSE,' shouted Vice Principal Hoovesly, **'IF RULES ARE BROKEN, THERE WILL BE SERIOUS CONSEQUENCES FOR THOSE WHO BREAK THEM!'**

I swallowed hard, my heart thumping. I'd seen Vice Principal Hoovesly go nutso before, but now he was losing the plot.

Out of the corner of my eye, I noticed that Squidge Dibley was scrunching up his face. His body was trembling.

'NOBODY,' growled Vice Principal Hoovesly, **'MAKES A FOOL OF –'**

At that moment a noise drowned out his words.

The most unlikely noise any of us expected to hear.

CHAPTER 25

t was the loudest, longest burp anybody had ever heard.

It was less of a **BURP**, and more of a **BUUUUUUUUUUUUUURP!**

It started like a foghorn. Then it morphed into a high-pitched squeal like air coming out of a balloon. After nine seconds it shifted into a trumpeting blast like a dying elephant. At thirteen seconds it got all squelchy sounding like someone stomping in mud. Then it went back to the foghorn sound again.

Vice Principal Hoovesly's face turned watermelon-red. His head quivered.

The burp kept going.

It chugged like a tractor for another ten long seconds, then it shifted again and became muffled as if the tractor were driving through water, then it went high pitched once more, but *really* high pitched like a mosquito was buzzing straight into a microphone.

And just as it seemed like it was about to run out of puff, it blasted louder, like someone had taped an amplifier to the butt cheeks of a buffalo that had eaten nothing but baked beans its whole life.

I thought that Vice Principal Hoovesly's head was going to explode. His jaw was vibrating. His finger-talons were digging into his skull.

BUT STILL THE BURP DIDN'T STOP.

Everyone looked around the room in shock, trying to work out where it was coming from. It seemed to be echoing from every wall.

The burp kept bellowing, loudly, then softly, then loudly again until finally, with one last spluttering pop like a dying engine, it conked out.

As it did, all eyes in the room turned to stare in disbelief at the perpetrator.

Squidge Dibley.

Vice Principal Hoovesly stood rigid, staring furiously at him. A thin trail of drool dripped from the edge of his open mouth.

I figured that this day was about to get ATOMICALLY BAD.

And it was only 9.15 in the morning.

'WHO. DO. YOU. THINK. YOU. ARE?!!!' screamed Vice Principal Hoovesly, towering over Squidge.

Everyone cowered backwards.

But not Squidge.

He just sat there looking at Vice Principal Hoovesly as if he were a big puppy dog and said, 'Squidge Dibley, at your service.'

CHAPTER 26

It was the first time Squidge had spoken. His voice was squeaky, like a talking chipmunk. He quietly unlatched his briefcase and took out an official-looking note. He handed it to me and squeakily whispered, 'Read? Out loud? But not loudly.'

I read the note out loud, but not loudly.

This is what it said:

To whom it may concern,
Squidge Dibley suffers from a rare medical condition known as NERVOUS BELLY BELCHUS.
Exposure to sudden loud noises such as shouting, yelling or angry outbursts will cause Squidge Dibley's stomach to violently

expel a surge of sulphuric stomach gases in the form of explosive burps and belches.

Big ones.

As there is no cure for NERVOUS BELLY BELCHUS, please do not shout or yell anywhere near Squidge Dibley.

Yours sincerely,

Dr Marcus Whalruss,

Craglands Institute of Burp Studies

Now I understood why Principal Shoutmouth had been whispering.

'NERVOUS BELLY BELCHUS?!' exclaimed Vice Principal Hoovesly, snatching the note from my hands.

'NERVOUS BELLY BELCHUS??!!!' he yelled again. Giant veins were throbbing in his temples. 'DO YOU EXPECT ME TO BELIEVE THAT THERE IS AN ACTUAL MEDICAL CONDITION CALLED NERVOUS BELLY BELCHUS??!!! WHAT ABSOLUTE NONSENSE!!'

Squidge burped again. Louder. Epically louder, and with such force that the tiny hairs that Vice

Principal Hoovesly kept plastered to his scalp stood up and started dancing like streamers on a fan.

The burp had so much G-force that Vice Principal Hoovesly skidded backwards across the carpet, crashing into Daniel Kwon-Yoon's desk. A stinky aroma filled the air like expired vanilla custard.

'HOW DARE YOU!!!' screeched Vice Principal Hoovesly.

Uh-oh, I thought. *He better stop shouting.* At the same time, I was desperate to see what would happen if he didn't.

Squidge burped again. Only, this burp was accompanied by a nasty gurgling, croaking sound from deep inside his stomach.

'Uh-oh,' said Daniel Kwon-Yoon. 'He's releasing a sequel.'

'Look out, sir!' yelled Crichton Peel, who had a perfect view of Squidge's face from the front of the classroom.

But it was **too late**.

Something lumpy and yellowish was spraying from Squidge's mouth. It looked like pancake mixture blended with rotten banana.

None of it missed Vice Principal Hoovesly. He was instantly transformed into a lumpy, yellow swamp monster.

Everyone screamed. Then everyone stopped screaming, remembering Squidge's medical note.

Vice Principal Hoovesly groaned and slipped backwards onto the floor. The yellow goop was in his ears, nose and mouth. He tried to wipe it from his face, but the more he wiped, the more it smeared all over him. He spluttered and hacked, little chunks of yellow moosh spraying from his lips.

'Farewell, breakfast,' whispered Squidge sadly to nobody in particular.

'That is messed up,' said Daniel Kwon-Yoon, trying not to gag.

Rebecca Peterson mouth trumpeted *The Last Post*.

'Water!' hissed Crichton Peel, running to help Vice Principal Hoovesly. 'He needs water!'

The Pritchard Twins handed Crichton some water. He sloshed it into Vice Principal Hoovesly's mouth. Only when it was half empty did Crichton realise that he'd been handed Bubble O'Gill's fish bowl.

Crichton yelped and accidentally dumped the rest of the water all over Vice Principal Hoovesly's head, covering his scalp with reeds and rainbow-coloured pebbles. He saw Crichton holding Bubble O'Gill's empty bowl.

Crichton backed away in fear.

He'd seen what we'd all seen: Bubble O'Gill's tail was hanging from Vice Principal Hoovesly's mouth.

CHAPTER 28

'**N**o!' cried Lenny Battisto. 'Not Bubble O'Gill!'

Vice Principal Hoovesly clutched his stomach. His body convulsed. He covered his mouth with both hands, but it was too late. His cheeks expanded and suddenly Bubble O'Gill shot out of his mouth like a spiky cannonball.

He sailed through the air, puffing up as he flew, and plonked onto Crichton's head with a wet PLOP.

'Nice hat,' said the Pritchard Twins.

Crichton shrieked and swiped Bubble O'Gill off his head. The little puffer fish catapulted upwards and ricocheted off the ceiling fan.

Everyone went crazy.

Even though he was our class mascot, nobody wanted Bubble O'Gill to touch them while he was covered in Vice Principal Hoovesly's stinky saliva. As he sailed over our heads, everybody charged out the door, knocking over chairs, tables and Vice Principal Hoovesly.

As I tumbled into the corridor, I glanced back and saw Squidge catching Bubble O'Gill safely in a jug of water.

The weird thing was that Squidge hadn't moved from his desk. He'd somehow managed to reach the exact spot where Bubble O'Gill was about to go splat on Lenny Battisto's desk, which was miles away from Squidge's.

How did he even do that?! I thought as I was carried away down the corridor by the rest of 6PU.

CHAPTER 29

Outside in the playground, the Year 5s were rehearsing their end-of-year musical, ESCAPE FROM ZOMBIE BAND CAMP.

It's about some kids in a school orchestra who get invited to perform a concert at a mysterious island resort, only to discover that they have been lured there by zombies to have their brains eaten.

I have to admit, it's a pretty epic plot. Tickets sold out fast.

They were right in the middle of practising the big final song – where the kids use their instruments as weapons to smash the zombies' heads off – so nobody noticed us spilling out into the playground. We ended up spending the rest of the morning playing zombie extras while the Year 5s rehearsed the song over and over. Squidge had now joined the rest of the class and sat cross legged, happily watching the whole performance.

None of us wanted to go back to class after recess, but the rehearsals were finished, so we had no choice.

Vice Principal Hoovesly was waiting for us. His face was yellow, and there were fronds of fishbowl weed stuck to his scalp.

As soon as we'd all sat down, he wrote a single word on the whiteboard:

'Laps?!!' gasped Rennie Grosse. 'Not laps!'

'Laps,' sneered Vice Principal Hoovesly, his glasses reflecting our horrified faces.

'But … the pool is closed,' whimpered Rennie. This was true. The pool had been closed for a week for emergency cleaning.

'Three. Hundred. Laps,' he added with sinister relish.

'Three hundred?!' whined Lenny Battisto.

'Three hundred and one,' said Vice Principal Hoovesly, smirking.

'Three hundred and one??!' blurted Daniel Kwon-Yoon.

'Three hundred and two,' said Vice Principal Hoovesly, inspecting his sharpened fingernails.

'Three hundred and two?!?!' groaned Shane Sloosman.

'Three hundred and three,' added Vice Principal Hoovesly.

Leanna Kingsley went to say, 'Three hundred and three?!' but we shushed her before we got more laps.

Silence fell across the room.

I looked over at Squidge Dibley. He was watching Bubble O'Gill circling around his tank.

The most laps we'd ever swum in a single session was forty, and that had taken an hour; three hundred and three laps would take forever.

Then I realised with relief that **NOBODY HAD THEIR SWIMMING GEAR WITH THEM!**

Vice Principal Hoovesly couldn't make us swim without it!

Or so we thought …

CHAPTER 30

If there was ever a moment that proved just how nasty Vice Principal Hoovesly was, this had to be it.

He made us wear swimming costumes from lost property!

He put Crichton in charge of handing them out.

It was horrible. They were all the wrong size, or too stretchy, or too loose. And there weren't enough boys' swimming shorts, so Rennie, Lenny and Shane all had to wear girls' swimming costumes.

There was a padlock on the gate of the pool and a big sign that said:

WARNING

DANGER

POOL CLOSED
FOR URGENT REPAIR

Vice Principal Hoovesly just unlocked it and herded us all in. The pool was dark green and smelled like compost. There was a family of ducks paddling in it.

I noticed a huge, angry-looking toad and a lump of floating feathers that looked like a dead ibis.

Vice Principal Hoovesly went to blow his whistle. He narrowed his eyes at Squidge, then blew the whistle quietly, right in our faces.

Nobody got in.

He blew his whistle again.

Still nobody got in.

His face was getting red now.

He went to blow his whistle again, then noticed someone standing in front of him.

It was Squidge Dibley. He was holding a note.

CHAPTER 31

Vice Principal Hoovesly snatched the note from Squidge and flung it to the ground without even reading it.

'EVERYBODY SWIMS!' he barked, spit flying from his mouth. 'NO EXCUSES!!!'

I thought Squidge was going to burp again, but before he could open his mouth, Vice Principal Hoovesly TOSSED HIM IN THE WATER!

Squidge landed in the dark green bilge with a plop and sank slowly, like the water was half-set jelly. It closed over the top of him, followed by the single blurp of an enormous bubble.

'That is *so* not wicked,' said the Pritchard Twins.

'It's seriously messed up,' whispered Daniel Kwon-Yoon.

'**EVERYBODY IN THE POOL, NOWWWW!!!**' screamed Vice Principal Hoovesly. '**AND IF YOU DON'T LIKE IT, JUST REMEMBER WHO IS IN CHARGE AROUND HERE ...**'

His voice trailed off.

A monstrous gurgling sound was coming from the pool.

'I've got a bad feeling about this ...' whimpered Rennie Grosse.

'Vice Principal Hoovesly! *Look*!' gasped Crichton Peel, pointing frantically at the pool.

The water level was dropping rapidly, as if the plug had been pulled from the bottom.

Squidge was nowhere to be seen, but the gurgling sound was growing louder.

Frightened animals were clambering out of the pool on every side. Ducks. Turtles. A sick-looking water rat.

Vice Principal Hoovesly peered into the water. He looked *nervous*, which was a new look for him. Angry, we'd seen plenty. Nasty, too. And vicious, most days. But never nervous.

Half the water was gone now. There was a scummy stain around the tiles where the water had been.

'What. Is. *That*?!' whispered Daniel Kwon-Yoon pointing at the middle of the pool.

CHAPTER 32

One of the hardest things about being the narrator of a story as freaky as Squidge Dibley's is that sometimes the things that happen are indescribable. Like, there aren't even words to explain them. But I'll try my best.

A big lump was rising out of the murky pool water, like the back of a whale. It was stripy. Or, it was *covered* in something stripy. The same stripy pattern as Squidge Dibley's shirt.

And it was growing.

It kept growing.

And growing.

We edged backwards, leaving Vice Principal Hoovesly staring dumbfounded into the pool.

I noticed a wet piece of paper at my feet. I picked it up, shaking off the water. It was Squidge's note. Rebecca Peterson read it out loud over my shoulder.

'To whom it may concern,
Please excuse Squidge Dibley from swimming on account of his rare condition known as
BLOATUS MAXIMUS.'

'Bloatus Maximus?!' echoed Shane Sloosman. 'What does that mean?'

'I think it means *that*!' said the Pritchard Twins, pointing at the pool.

The big stripy lump had grown into a massive, watermelon shape the size of a bus.

Rebecca continued reading the note.

'Under no circumstances should Squidge be fully submerged in water, as his BLOATUS MAXIMUS will cause him to absorb all liquid in contact with his body. He will expand like a massive sponge until he is fifty times his normal size.

Yours courteously,
Professor Geraldine McSnorkell,
Craglands Institute of Marine Maladies'

All the pool water was gone now, replaced by an enormous, swollen Squidge. He was the size of a blue whale.

'Wicked,' said the Pritchard Twins.

'Epic,' said Daniel Kwon-Yoon.

We had **no idea** what was going to happen next. If we had known, we would have filmed it for sure, because it would now be the most-watched video of all time.

CHAPTER 33

Vice Principal Hoovesly stared up at Squidge and screamed, **'DIBLEY! YOU PUT THAT WATER BACK. NOW!!!'**

Crichton Peel poked Squidge with a pool scoop.

Squidge laughed giddily, his arms flopping around like eels.

'DIBLEY!' yelled Vice Principal Hoovesly, kicking a duck out of the way. **'I'M GOING TO COUNT TO THR—'**

He never made it to the end of the word because at that moment, Crichton jabbed Squidge again, harder this time, and Squidge *exploded*.

Well, not really, but that's what it looked like.

At exactly the same moment as Crichton jammed the pool scoop into Squidge's swollen body, an explosive spray of chunky, green water sprayed out of Squidge's nostrils, hitting Vice Principal Hoovesly and Crichton like a horizontal volcano, and sending them flying out the gate.

Squidge deflated fast, the green geysers gushing from his nose. Vice Principal Hoovesly and Crichton disappeared across the road towards the school.

'That. Was. Epic!' said Daniel Kwon-Yoon.

'Wicked,' said the Pritchard Twins.

Squidge lay on the bottom of the empty pool, surrounded by unhappy tadpoles. He sneezed sheepishly.

I was starting to understand what made Squidge so special. And how he had stretched up to the third-storey window. As far as I could tell, he was half human, half elastic.

'I guess squad training is over,' chuckled Abigail Takani, opening yet another sugar sachet.

We carried Squidge back to school on our shoulders. His body was so stretched, he was like a rubber anaconda.

'You are one weird dude, dude,' said Daniel Kwon-Yoon. 'You're like a human Gummi Bear.'

'Yeah,' said Leanna Kingsley, bringing up the rear. 'My dad works for NASA, and if you ask me, you're definitely an alien.'

'Alien?' said Lenny Battisto. 'I'm scared.'

'He's not an alien,' I said. 'He's just … Squidge.'

None of us understood exactly what made Squidge the way he was, but as far as we were concerned, he was exactly what we had been waiting for to rescue us from Vice Principal Hoovesly's reign of horror.

As we scurried across the playground, we heard Principal Shoutmouth yelling from her private bathroom.

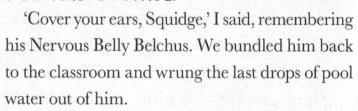

'VICE PRINCIPAL HOOVESLY! HOW **DARE YOU** BURST INTO MY LAVATORY DURING **MY** ABLUTIONS! I EXPECT A THOROUGH EXPLANATION FOR THIS OUTRAGE!'

'Cover your ears, Squidge,' I said, remembering his Nervous Belly Belchus. We bundled him back to the classroom and wrung the last drops of pool water out of him.

Then, as we all gathered around, Squidge told us the story about how he was born.

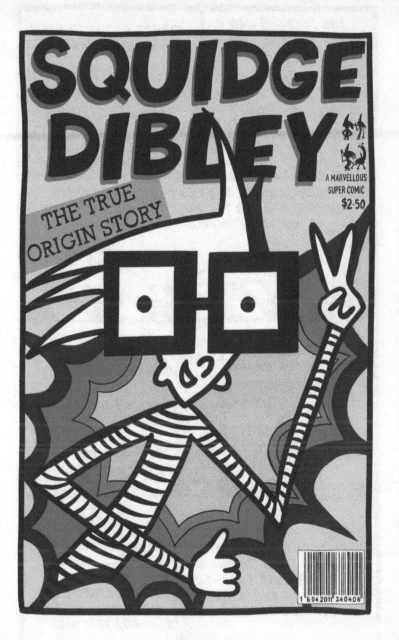

THE DOCTORS HAD NEVER SEEN ANYTHING LIKE IT.

NOBODY HAD EVER SEEN ANYTHING LIKE IT.

WHEN SQUIDGE ARRIVED IN THE WORLD, HE BOUNCED AROUND THE HOSPITAL WALLS LIKE AN OUT-OF-CONTROL SQUASH BALL.

HE LANDED IN A BASIN AND GOT STUCK IN THE DRAIN.

WHEN THEY TRIED TO PULL HIM FREE, HE STRETCHED OUT LIKE A BUNGEE.

THEY THOUGHT THEY'D PERMANENTLY ELONGATED HIM, BUT TO EVERYONE'S SHOCK HE JUST SNAPPED BACK INTO SHAPE AND GURGLED HAPPILY.

THE DOCTORS KEPT HIM IN THE HOSPITAL FOR TESTING.

EXTRA DOCTORS WERE CALLED IN.

SPECIALISTS WERE CALLED IN.

EXTRA SPECIALIST DOCTORS WERE CALLED IN.

BUT NOBODY HAD ANY CLUE WHY THIS BRAND-NEW BABY WAS SO STRETCHY, SQUASHY AND, WELL ... SQUIDGY.

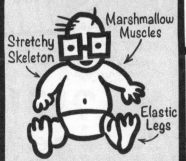

Marshmallow Muscles

Stretchy Skeleton

Elastic Legs

HIS PARENTS DIDN'T CARE. THEY'D NEVER BEEN EXACTLY NORMAL THEMSELVES.

AND IF THEIR SON HAPPENED TO BE SQUIDGIER THAN OTHER BABIES, WELL, THAT WAS NO BIG DEAL TO THEM.

NOTHING COULD STOP THEM LOVING HIM.

SO, THEY CALLED HIM

SQUIDGE

THEY STOPPED WORRYING ABOUT WHY HE WAS THE WAY HE WAS —

THOUGH HIS MUM SECRETLY WONDERED IF IT WAS BECAUSE SHE'D EATEN NOTHING BUT CRUMBED CALAMARI RINGS AND JELLY SNAKES THE ENTIRE TIME HE WAS IN HER BELLY.

Jelly Snakes

THEY DID THEIR BEST TO HELP SQUIDGE FIT INTO THE WORLD.

EXCEPT THAT THE WORLD WASN'T READY FOR SQUIDGE ...

?!?!

THEIR LOCAL SCHOOL WAS CRAGLANDS WEST MILITARY COLLEGE.

THE BUILDING USED TO BE A PRISON. IT WAS ABOUT THE GLOOMIEST SCHOOL ON EARTH.

THE TEACHERS DIDN'T KNOW WHAT TO DO WITH SQUIDGE. HE WAS TOO STRETCHY AND STRANGE FOR ALL THEIR STRICT RULES.

IN THE END, THEY WRAPPED HIM IN SPONGES AND KEPT HIM IN A CLASSROOM WITH PADDED WALLS IN CASE HIS STRETCHINESS CAUSED AN ACCIDENT.

AT THE MILITARY COLLEGE, SQUIDGE FELT SQUASHED.

THEN ONE DAY A NEW TEACHER CAME TO THE COLLEGE.

HE'D NEVER MET A TEACHER LIKE HER. SHE TREATED HIM LIKE A REGULAR KID. ONLY BETTER.

SHE SET HIM FREE FROM HIS FOAM CLASSROOM AND ENCOURAGED HIM TO STRETCH HIMSELF TO HIS FULL POTENTIAL.

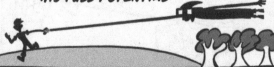

SQUIDGE LOVED THE TEACHER AND THE TEACHER LOVED SQUIDGE –

EVEN IF SOMETIMES HE GOT INTO SOME STICKY SITUATIONS.

SHE EVEN GAVE HIM A NICKNAME

DIBS

BUT THEN LAST YEAR THE TEACHER GOT TRANSFERRED AWAY FROM THE MILITARY COLLEGE.

Bye

SQUIDGE WAS PUT BACK IN HIS SPECIAL ROOM AND TOLD NOT TO DO ANYTHING SQUIDGY.

SO, FINALLY HIS MUM AND DAD DECIDED THAT THE ONLY WAY FOR SQUIDGE TO GROW UP LIKE A NORMAL KID WAS TO GO TO A NORMAL SCHOOL.

AND THAT'S HOW HE ENDED UP AT CRAGLANDS SOUTH PRIMARY.

CHAPTER 34

Vice Principal Hoovesly crashed through the classroom door, covered in green pool bilge. A frog jumped out of his pocket. He slowly straightened his tie and squelched towards Squidge.

'Nobody makes a **fOOL** of Hector Hoovesly,' he whispered.

'Your name is Hector?' asked Squidge, brightly.

'What?' hissed Vice Principal Hoovesly.

'I had a hamster called Hector,' continued Squidge. 'But he crawled into the toaster and got toasted. Then the dog ate him. Poor Hector.'

'I DON'T CARE ABOUT YOUR STUPID TOASTED HAMSTER!' bellowed Vice Principal Hoovesly, his nose virtually touching Squidge's. He stopped suddenly, realising too late that he had shouted.

A *squealing, gurgling* sound echoed from deep inside Squidge's stomach.

Everyone cowered under their desks.

'No!' shouted Vice Principal Hoovesly. 'Not again!!!'

The gurgling from Squidge's stomach rumbled like an earthquake. Vice Principal Hoovesly *pulled him out of his chair with one hand* and held him aloft.

'OUT!' he screamed. **'OUT OF MY CLASSROOM!'**

I couldn't believe what happened next.

He swung Squidge around and around and hurled him through the air towards the front window!

'Whoa!' said Abigail Takani, as Squidge soared, tummy gurgling, over our heads. 'I thought things like this only happened in books.'

But just as it looked like he was about to crash right through the window, Squidge tucked his knees into his chest, expanded into a perfect sphere and bounced right off the window frame like a jumbo basketball.

He ricocheted from wall to wall, crashing into every single portrait of Vice Principal Hoovesly, smashing them to pieces. We watched in awe as he **bounced** and **rebounded** and **bounced** and **rebounded** around the room until finally he crashed into Vice Principal Hoovesly's rule board. It fell to the floor and split in half.

The room was a mess.

Squidge rolled slowly to a stop and hiccupped.

'WHAT. HAVE. YOU. DONE. TO. MY. CLASSROOM?!' seethed Vice Principal Hoovesly looking at the destruction around him.

Squidge unlatched his briefcase and handed Vice Principal Hoovesly a note. It read:

To whom it may concern,
Squidge Dibley suffers from a rare condition known as BUNGEE BONES. If he comes into contact with a hard surface at high speed, he will lose control of his movement and bounce erratically until gravity slows him down.
It is unlikely that he will be harmed.
Please do not hold him responsible for any accidental damage he causes to property.
Yours sincerely,
Dr Robert Bogonnheim,
Craglands Institute of Skeletal Abnormalities

'BUNGEE BONES?' growled Vice Principal Hoovesly, crumpling the note. 'BUNGEE BONES?! I'LL GIVE YOU BUNGEE BONES! I WANT YOU OUT OF THIS SCHOOL! NOW!'

Hoovesly grabbed Squidge again, but this time we were ready. We grabbed Squidge's legs and pulled him backwards.

'I'll help, sir!' said Crichton Peel, grabbing one of Squidge's arms and pulling him towards the door.

It was a Squidge tug-o-war. I thought he was going to rip in half, but he stretched and stretched until finally there was an enormous *TWANG!* Vice Principal Hoovesly and Crichton were flung backwards, their butts smashing through the back wall of the classroom.

We heard screams from Mrs Kinetty's Kindergarten class next door at the sight of two unidentified butts poking through the wall.

'That is messed up,' said Daniel Kwon-Yoon over the sounds of the crying Kindergarten kids.

Squidge twanged back to half his normal size. He looked like an accordion, but he didn't seem worried about what was happening.

'You are wicked,' said the Pritchard Twins.

'NOBODY MAKES A FOOL OF HECTOR HOOVESLY!!!' snarled Vice Principal Hoovesly, ripping himself out of the wall and storming towards Squidge.

Squidge started giggling. Everyone thought he was crazy. Then we saw what he was laughing about.

The back of
Vice Principal
Hoovesly's pants
had ripped wide open.

His underpants were
covered in flowers.
**'EEK! MY
PANTALOONS!'**
he bellowed at the
top of his voice.

Squidge burped
loudly, smiled and took
out the note about his
NERVOUS BELLY BELCHUS from his briefcase.

Vice Principal Hoovesly tore the note to pieces
and let out a long, loud, frustrated wail like a
constipated camel.

Squidge burped again. Vice Principal Hoovesly
shook his fist in the air and screamed, **'I'VE HAD
IT, DIBLEY!'**

What happened next, happened fast.

CHAPTER 35

Vice Principal Hoovesly grabbed Squidge and stomped towards the very same window I'd first seen Squidge at just that morning.

'Uh-oh,' said Leanna Kingsley. 'He's going to launch him into orbit.'

Squidge gripped the edges of the window frame. Unlike all of us, he didn't seem the slightest bit scared of Vice Principal Hoovesly, or worried that this crazy, talon-fingered freak was about to fling him out the window.

'I'LL GIVE YOU **BUNGEE BONES**,' said Vice Principal Hoovesly, pulling Squidge's body backwards like a human slingshot. **'YOU'RE EXPELLED!!!'**

He let go, and Squidge fired out into the sky.

'Whoa!' said Daniel Kwon-Yoon.

We ran to the window and watched in horror as Squidge disappeared up into the sky.

'**WHAT. IS. GOING. ON. HERE?!**' hissed a voice from the doorway.

It was Principal Shoutmouth.

She surveyed the wreckage of the classroom. The smashed portraits. The butt-shaped hole in the back wall next to where Crichton Peel was still stuck in the plasterboard.

Then she saw Vice Principal Hoovesly's underpants.

'VICE **PRINCIPAL!** WHAT HAPPENED TO YOUR SLACKS?!' she asked. 'AND **WHY** ARE YOUR STUDENTS LOOKING OUT THE WINDOW, WHEN THEY SHOULD BE LOOKING AT THEIR **TEXTBOOKS?**'

'Ah, heh heh,' laughed Vice Principal Hoovesly nervously, his face darting between the doorway and the windows.

Principal Shoutmouth shuffled to the front window and poked her head out.

Squidge was soaring into the clouds like a missile.

'VICE PRINCIPAL HOOVESLY!!!'

shouted Principal Shoutmouth. **'I PUT YOU IN CHARGE OF A STUDENT REQUIRING SPECIAL CARE! WHY IS HE CURRENTLY FLYING INTO THE STRATOSPHERE?!'**

'Errr …' said Vice Principal Hoovesly, sweat dripping down his face. 'Mr Dibley … tripped.'

'TRIPPED?' shouted Principal Shoutmouth. **'TRIPPED?!!!'**

Squidge was just a dot in the sky now.

Principal Shoutmouth jabbed a finger at Vice Principal Hoovesly's chest and shouted, **'IF YOU DO NOT CATCH SQUIDGE DIBLEY, YOU WILL NEVER SET FOOT INSIDE THIS SCHOOL EVER AGAIN!'**

'Ever?' we all said, hopefully. It was too good to be true.

This could be our chance!

CHAPTER 36

Vice Principal Hoovesly bolted from the room and appeared down in the playground a moment later, his flowery undies showing through the rip in his pants. He grabbed the pool scoop that Crichton had dropped during their ride on the river of pool bilge. He held it up and looked into the sky.

The Squidge dot was falling back down now.

'Err ... I've got you, Dibley,' called Vice
Principal Hoovesly, scurrying back and forth like
a scared crab. 'Everything will be okay. Just land
in this net, lad!'

Abigail Takani said it first. Just a peep, really,
barely audible: 'Miss!'

'Miss!' echoed Lenny Battisto.

'Miss!' said the Pritchard Twins.

The chant caught on quick.

'Miss! Miss! Miss! Miss!' we yelled as Vice
Principal Hoovesly ran in circles around the
playground, pool scoop poised for the catch.

We figured that with his BUNGEE BONES,

Squidge would bounce down safely. We just didn't want Vice Principal Hoovesly to catch him. It was the only way we'd be free of him forever.

The Squidge dot was getting bigger, his arms and legs flapping as he plummeted towards the school.

We chanted louder.

'MISS! MISS! **MISS!**' **'DON'T YOU DARE MISS!'** shouted Principal Shoutmouth.

Vice Principal Hoovesly danced frantically from side to side.

'Listen, guys,' I whispered. 'We have to help Squidge!'

'But what can we do?' asked Shane Sloosman.

It was a good question. I looked around at my 6PU classmates. Okay, we were a bunch of weirdos. But maybe that was our strength. Wasn't it?

Then, I had an idea.

CHAPTER 37

As we peered down at Vice Principal Hoovesly from our third-storey classroom, a plan came together in my head. A big, ridiculous, crazy plan.

A plan even crazier than any of the crazy plans my dad had ever had for his crazy businesses. But a plan that I figured might be *just* crazy enough to work.

'Daniel,' I said. 'We need a skateboard.'

'Which one?' replied Daniel Kwon-Yoon, producing three skateboards he had hidden behind a bookshelf.

'Whichever is the gnarliest,' I said.

'Behold, the Thunder Beast,' said Daniel.

'That'll do it,' I said.

I turned to the Pritchard twins. 'Do you two have some kind of slingshot? A big one?'

'Like this?' asked the Pritchard Twins, pulling out an enormous monster of a slingshot that was hidden under their desk.

'Perfect!' I said, turning to Leanna Kingsley. 'Leanna. We need your launching skills.'

'My dad does work for NASA, you know,' she said.

'Nathan,' I said. 'Get some paint.'

'Yes!' said Nathan Kobeissi, pumping his fist.

'Rebecca, stand by to blast your trumpet.'

'Standing by,' said Rebecca Peterson, holding her trumpet to her mouth.

'Hurry, Padman!' urged Lenny Battisto, clutching the window frame. 'Squidge is falling fast.'

Vice Principal Hoovesly was walking slowly backwards, perfectly positioned to catch Squidge.

'Rebecca! Cue the trumpet!' I said. 'Nathan, load the paint.'

Nathan dumped a whole bottle of paint into Rebecca's trumpet.

'Let's paint Hoovesly's head with music!' I said.

Rebecca took a huge breath, pointed the trumpet out the window and blew.

An ear-splitting honk echoed through the school as a giant ball of brown paint flew high up in the air above Vice Principal Hoovesly.

I turned to Daniel, Leanna and the Pritchard Twins.

'Launch the Thunder Beast!' I said. 'Target Hoovesly's hooves.'

They loaded Daniel's skateboard into the giant slingshot.

'Target acquired,' said the Pritchard Twins, looking out the window at Vice Principal Hoovesly's feet.

'Readjust launch trajectory by point zero three five,' said Leanna Kingsley, nudging the giant elastic to the left. 'And … fire!'

They released the slingshot. Daniel's skateboard sliced through the air towards Vice Principal Hoovesly.

'VICE PRINCIPAL HOOVESLY!' yelled Crichton, still stuck in the back wall of the classroom. 'LOOK OU—'

He was cut short as Bubble O'Gill burst out of his bowl and straight into Crichton's mouth.

'That is one freaky fish,' said Daniel Kwon-Yoon.

Vice Principal Hoovesly's face was splattered with brown paint. He jumped in the air in shock.

'**yes!**' we cheered.

The Thunder Beast slid right beneath his flailing legs. He landed on it heavily and careened across the playground, screaming and juggling the pool scoop blindly.

Suddenly, the skateboard hit a bench, catapulting Vice Principal Hoovesly straight up into the air.

'Hoovesly, you have a problem,' said Leanna Kingsley as Vice Principal Hoovesly fired upwards, past our window.

'Ten bucks says he crash-lands on the library,' said the Pritchard Twins.

'No way,' said Lenny Battisto. 'He's going to hit the canteen, for sure.'

'Basketball courts, I say,' said Leanna Kingsley. 'My dad works for NASA, so I can tell.'

'Whatever he hits, he'll be paying for the damage,' said Principal Shoutmouth looking at us all with her arms folded.

Uh-oh, I thought. I'd forgotten she was watching from the other window. We were seriously in for it.

'6PU!' she continued, staring at our guilty faces. A smile formed on her lips and she added,

'I believe that a situation like this calls for a countdown.'

Leanna Kingsley started counting down. We all joined in as Vice Principal Hoovesly dropped faster and faster.

'Ten, nine, eight, seven, six, five, four, three, two, one – **OOOOhhhhh!!!!**'

One end of the pool scoop crashed into the roof of the library with a **CRUNCH**. The other hit the roof of the canteen, wedging Vice Principal Hoovesly between the two buildings.

Everyone cheered.

Vice Principal Hoovesly groaned.

'That's gotta hurt,' said Shane Sloosman.

'THAT WAS THE MOST **AWESOME THING I HAVE EVER SEEN!**' yelled Abigail Takani in full sugar-rush mode.

Vice Principal Hoovesly sat motionless on the pole, whimpering. Then he slowly rotated upside down.

A bird landed on the pole next to him. Then another. And another. Then a giant ibis flapped in and clung to Vice Principal Hoovesly's head.

'Now *that* is a work of art,' said the Pritchard Twins.

Even Principal Shoutmouth quietly chuckled.

'Wait a minute,' I said, looking up at the sky. 'Where's Squidge?'

'Squidge is right here, where he belongs,' said a voice from the doorway. Standing there was Ms Trigley with Squidge sitting on her shoulders. They were both smiling.

CHAPTER 38

'**S**he caught me,' squeaked Squidge, looking down happily at Ms Trigley.

'Just like old times, Dibs,' said Ms Trigley.

'**MS TRIGLEY!**' we cried, swarming around her. 'You're back!!!'

'Sorry I had to leave you, nutjobs,' she said. 'I haven't been feeling too well.'

'*You're* Squidge's old teacher?' I asked. 'From the military college?'

'Dibs and I go way back,' said Ms Trigley. 'But teachers get transferred all over the place, so I had to go wherever they sent me.'

Then we noticed her tummy.

157

'You're **FAT!**' said Lenny Battisto, pointing at her belly.

'She's not fat,' said the Pritchard Twins.

'She is!' said Lenny. 'Look at her belly. It's **ENORMOUS!**'

'That's because there's a baby in it, you nitwit,' said the Pritchard Twins.

'What?!' cried Lenny. 'How did a baby get in there?!'

'Stop talking now,' said the Pritchard Twins.

The next ten minutes were spent hugging and celebrating Ms Trigley's return. It turned out that her sudden departure from the school had nothing to do with the disastrous Speech Slam incident. The bear trap hadn't even hurt her at all, thanks to her indestructible army boots. It was actually Vice Principal Hoovesly who insisted that she be driven away in an ambulance.

She explained that the real problem was that she had a super bad case of something called morning sickness, which sometimes happens when people have a baby in their tummy. And that the longer the baby was in her tummy, the more gurgly she felt.

'Her fault for swallowing one,' whispered Lenny Battisto.

But when Ms Trigley had heard that Squidge was going to transfer into her class at Craglands South, she was determined to come back as soon as she felt better. There was no way she was going to miss Squidge's first day.

'Sorry I'm a bit late, Dibs,' she said.

'Peculiar,' said Principal Shoutmouth. 'Vice Principal Hoovesly informed me that you'd asked for the rest of the year off due to the injuries you sustained during the bear-trap incident.'

'I've had worse bites from my pet rats,' chuckled Ms Trigley.

Then we told them both all the awful stuff that Vice Principal Hoovesly had done and how horrible it had been. Principal Shoutmouth listened quietly, taking notes.

Even Crichton joined in, admitting that Vice Principal Hoovesly had been a pretty terrible teacher, even if Crichton had been his number one accomplice.

'I suppose we had better get him before those birds do,' said Principal Shoutmouth eventually, looking out the front window again.

CHAPTER 39

'The kids told me everything, Vice Principal,' yelled Principal Shoutmouth over the flock of squawking birds nesting on him. 'I know what you've been up to!'

'**Lies!**' screeched Vice Principal Hoovesly. 'All children are liars! I will not tolerate lies in my classroom!'

'Not your classroom anymore, H-bomb,' called Ms Trigley. 'These nutjobs are my kids again.'

Vice Principal Hoovesly glowered at her and yelled, 'Nobody makes a fool of Hector Hoovesly!'

'Hector?' echoed Ms Trigley, looking at Squidge. 'Didn't you have a toasted hamster called Hector?'

'I DON'T WANT TO HEAR ABOUT HIS STUPID TOASTED HAMSTER!' yelled Vice Principal Hoovesly. He was about to say more when the enormous ibis stuck its beak in his open mouth and regurgitated a lump of chewed-up worms straight down his throat.

'GROSS!!!' yelled everybody.

'This school is so messed up,' said Daniel Kwon-Yoon.

At that moment, a possum crept out from the roof of the canteen and scuttled nervously onto the pool scoop.

It was followed by another and another, until there was a whole family of possums crossing from one building to the next. The pool scoop began to bend under their weight.

'A-HA!' yelled a voice from the library roof. It was the school maintenance lady, Ms Bromley.

'Where did *she* come from?!' asked Lenny.

'Now I've got you, you feral furballs!' she shrieked.

She had burst up through the roof, covered in

cobwebs. Roof tiles were flying everywhere as she aimed an enormous DIY catapult at the startled possums.

'I'VE BEEN WAITING IN THAT ROOF FOR SIX WEEKS FOR YOU PESTS TO COME OUT!' she cackled, slowly pulling back the catapult.

'MS BROMLEY! WAIT!' shouted Principal Shoutmouth.

THWANG!!! went the catapult, firing a net through the air towards the startled possums. The arm of the catapult bounced back, conking Ms Bromley on the head.

'EEEEEEEK!' she screamed, tumbling backwards and crashing straight through the ceiling below.

The frightened birds scattered into the air. The possums clung on for their lives.

The pool scoop handle broke in half.

Vice Principal Hoovesly hung in the air for a nanosecond, his face terrified.

Then he fell.

Just as he was about to hit the asphalt, Squidge dived out the window and made his body into a balloon-shaped safety mat.

Vice Principal Hoovesly bounced off Squidge, sailed through the air and landed in Kindergarten's vegetable garden with an enormous PLOP!

It was the most *epic* thing anybody had ever witnessed at Craglands South Primary.

CHAPTER 40

Things calmed down a lot after that.

Ms Trigley took over the class again. She got rid of all traces of Vice Principal Hoovesly, including his rules.

She made Squidge the honorary class captain for showing **epic bravery** and **extreme elasticity** in the face of adversity.

Crichton protested that HE was class captain, but he backed down when Ms Trigley asked him if he wanted to go back to being Vice Principal Hoovesly's sidekick.

Crichton didn't say anything after that. Not that he could be Vice Principal Hoovesly's sidekick anyway.

Vice Principal Hoovesly wasn't vice principal anymore.

When Ms Bromley had fallen back through the ceiling during her possum-catching operation, she broke seventy-five bones. She was going to be in hospital for at least a year.

Principal Shoutmouth said that if Vice Principal Hoovesly wanted to stay at Craglands South Primary, he would have to take over Ms Bromley's job.

So, now he is Janitor Hoovesly.

He can't even give us any detentions. And he had to give back EVERYTHING he had confiscated over the years.

And Ms Trigley is the new vice principal! So, all in all, things have turned out okay. I even found out that Squidge **LOVES curry!** Like seriously, **LOVES** it! And it doesn't make him fart.

So, we swap lunch every day and he comes over to my place after school all the time, which is awesome because he's seriously into building stuff out of junk.

Dad says he might make Squidge and me official employees in his new 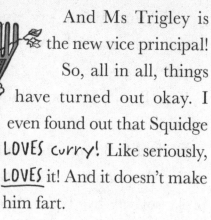 inventing business.

So far Squidge has invented **gelato-flavoured paint** that you can actually eat (Nathan Kobeissi loves it);

a **remote-control scorpion**, which he gave to Daniel Kwon-Yoon as a pet;

a **trumpet-playing robot**, so now Rebecca Peterson can play duets;

a massive **aquarium maze** for Bubble O'Gill;

and a **pencil case that absorbs fart smells.**

Everyone is especially grateful for that one. Squidge even built a machine called an **ultrasound**, which is a kind of X-ray camera for looking inside tummies, which means we have been able to get to know Ms Trigley's baby before it is even born.

And get this – we **WON** the **ANNUAL JUNIOR REGIONAL WATER WAR** against Craglands North Private, because Squidge was faster than every one of their swimmers.

Maybe it wasn't fair that he stretched all the way to the end of the pool without even getting in the water, but everyone agreed that his athleticism deserved to be acknowledged.

Janitor Hoovesly tried to take all the credit, of course.

CHAPTER 41

But the very best thing about everything that happened is that nobody calls me Pad anymore. Squidge gave me a new nickname: **POD**. It's a short way of saying Padman O'Donnell.

He thought of it when we went on an excursion to Leanna Kingsley's dad's work. Turns out that he actually does work for NASA. Well, sort of.

Even Mum and Dad call me Pod now. And I kind of like it!

We finally had the **Speech Slam** and I came **First**. Everyone thought Dad's fossilised cat was epic, and after my speech, Ms Trigley told me that I'd make a really good narrator for a story.

That's how I ended up telling this story. The story of how Squidge Dibley destroyed the school – for Vice Principal Hoovesly, anyway – and made everything better. It took months to write it all down, and some of my drawings are a bit wobbly, but Ms Trigley says that's okay because life isn't meant to be all perfect and normal.

She says the best things in the world are definitely a little bit squidgy.

Excellent work, Pod.
$\frac{10}{10}$ But are my legs
REALLY that hairy?!
Ms. T